Sheltered

Coleen Misher

Contents

1.

"Honey, it's time to get up," I hear my mama say softly.

"Mhm, I'm up," I reply in a scratchy voice.

"I'm going to be making breakfast. Be dressed and downstairs in ten minutes." I hear her leave my room.

I lay there for a couple more minutes before getting up. I walk to my closet and pick out my favorite dress. It's pink and is just above my knees. It's sleeves don't really cover my shoulders so I slip on a jean jacket. I then put on flats. I spin in the mirror two times to admire my outfit.

I smile as I brush my blonde hair. My mama has light brown hair, but she told me that my hair is similar to my daddy's hair. I haven't ever met him, but my mama says I don't want to. I never asked why that is even though I'm really curious. My mama also said I have his light hazel eyes which I'm glad for cause I love my eyes.

My mama said my daddy left us when I was only one and a half. She always says that it's a good thing he did. I've asked why a few times, but she's only said that it's because he was a mess. I'm not allowed to ask about him, but it's hard not to. I sigh as I set my hair brush down then make my way downstairs.

"Is that all you're going to wear? It doesn't cover much." My mama looks at my outfit.

"I didn't think about it. I'll go put on some socks." I turn around and go upstairs.

I change into socks that reach the middle of my calf. I pull them up then put my flats back on. I look at my outfit and smile. I'm not trying to be vain or anything, but I think I look good. I've always liked the way I look which may sound conceited, but I really don't know why I can't love myself. I walk back downstairs and my mama grins.

"That's better, sweetie." She's already put the plates on the table so I sit down.

"So, what are we doing today?" I take a bite of my toast.

"Since it's Saturday, I thought about going to the market. I need some eggs and bagels."

"Oh okay. I think we're almost out of jam, too." I look at her.

"I'll have to get some strawberries then."

"Can I help make it?" I ask her hopefully.

"Of course." She smiles.

We continue eating in silence, but that silence is interrupted when we hear a scream from outside. I drop my fork and it clatters to the ground. My mama doesn't even look fazed, but I want to know what's going on so I get up and go look at the window. There's an older female and older male running around in the next door neighbor's lawn with goofy grins on their faces. They look really happy and I watch them for another minute before going back to the table.

"You shouldn't spy on people like that, Maureen. It isn't kind." My mama scolds.

"I'm sorry, mama. I was just curious." I defend myself as I pick my fork up. I then grab my nearly empty plate and scrape the remaining food into the trash.

"Go brush your teeth. I'm leaving in five." I nod then head back upstairs.

I didn't tell you before, but my room isn't exactly on the second story of the house. The house has two other bedrooms besides my mama's room, but one of them is the sewing room and the other is where I do my schoolwork. I'm home schooled because my mama doesn't trust public schools. She prefers teaching me on her own. We sew most of our own clothes, but sometimes we go out and buy clothes.

There's four steps that lead to my room. My room used to be the attic, but my mama turned it into a bedroom. It's pretty big and it could probably be a small apartment to some people. I have my own bathroom which is really nice in my opinion. My mama wasn't sure about putting a bathroom in my room because it would be the only door I could lock.

I even have an almost full wall of bookshelves. There's just enough room on the walls for two small windows. I also have a bay window with a nice cushioned seat. I like sitting and reading on it for hours at a time. It's my favorite part of my room.

I hurry and brush my teeth. I run back downstairs quickly. My mama is on the phone when I get down there. I don't reveal myself just yet in case it's a private conversation. I do however listen when I hear the next three sentences that leave her mouth.

"You're immature people who need to grow up. You have four children, Mrs. Kinsley. I have one child and she doesn't need you and your family creating chaos outside our window, understood?" My mama practically yells into the phone.

I decide to make my presence known by coughing. My mama turns around quickly with an annoyed look on her face. I don't know why she's so angry at Mrs. Kinsley. I thought it was amusing to watch her and her husband having fun.

"I have to go, but please be thoughtful of your actions next time." She hangs up the phone abruptly.

"Ready to go, mama?" I smile which makes her anger disappear.

"Yeah, let's go." She grabs her keys and I follow her outside.

We have a garage, but my mama prefers parking the car on the driveway. She uses the garage for storage since she can't use the attic. We only have one car which is all we need since I don't even know how to drive. I'm seventeen, but my mama says I don't need my license. I wish she would change her mind about that.

I get in the car and notice a girl in the neighbor's yard. She has black hair that reaches the middle of her back. I can only see the side of her, but I can tell she's laughing. Her parents are spraying each other with the hose and laughing. I see two younger kids with small containers of water who are trying to get each other soaked. Right as I put my seatbelt on, the girl looks at me and something inside of me flutters.

"Gosh, who let's their daughter dress and look like that?" I can tell my mama disapproves, but I don't know if I can agree with her.

2.

I can't stop picturing that girl. She's all I think about on the way to the market. I love her jade green eyes that practically sparkled in the sunlight. She was pale, but the rest of her family looks a little bit tanner than her. She also had two visible piercings which I know my mama would dislike. My mama hates that kind of stuff.

We've been neighbors with them my whole life. I've never really seen the girl before. She rarely seems to go outside unlike the rest of her family. I know there's two younger siblings and an older brother. The parents are young and full of energy like the younger two.

We get to the market and my mama grabs her purse before getting out. I follow behind her like always. I keep my head down to avoid any eye contact. We walk in the market and I look up so I don't run into people. My mama gets two baskets then hands me one.

"We only need a couple things. Can you go get the strawberries?" She asks.

"Sure." I head towards the strawberries.

"Can I help you with anything?" An older boy asks with a smirk. I realize it's the brother of that girl.

He has bright red hair which isn't similar to any of his family members. I know he's dyed it. His eyes are similar to his sisters, but a bit blueish like his daddy's eyes. His arms are covered in tattoos which is also another thing he has in common with his daddy. The only thing he has similar with his mama is his nose like the rest of the children.

"Nope. Thank you for asking, though." I reply with a small smile. I start looking through the strawberries to see which ones are good and which ones are bad.

"You live next door, right?" He's standing close to me.

"Yes." I continue looking.

"I'm Raphael. I don't think we've ever actually met."

"Maureen. My mama likes us to keep to ourselves."

"So she's controlling?" He grins and I roll my eyes.

"No. Just protective." I want him to go away, but I know he won't.

"Mhm, sure she is." He smirks and I glare at him.

"You're being a bit nosy." I tell him with a glare.

"Sorry. I don't mean to be."

"Maureen, you ready?" I look to see my mama. I've picked out the necessary strawberry amount so I nod.

"Hi, Mrs. Baker." The boy says with a friendly grin.

"Hello. C'mon, Maureen. We have a busy day ahead of us."

I follow my mama to the check out lanes. We get the same older lady from last time. She's fast, but extremely talkative. My mama answers the questions in a fake tone. She obviously doesn't care at all, but the lady doesn't seem to notice. I feel bad for her, but I don't know what to do.

"Have a nice day," The lady says, but my mama doesn't respond this time.

"Thanks. You too." I smile as I follow behind my mama.

"She was too talkative. She may be fast, but she needs to learn to shut it." She says as we leave the market.

"She's just really friendly. You should be more appreciative of people like that, mama." I reply.

"Don't tell me what I should and shouldn't do, Maureen." She gives me a disapproving look as she unlocks the car.

"Sorry." I set the groceries in the back of the car. She does the same then we get in and leave.

□*□*□*□

"That should last us another month," My mama tells me as she sets one of the jars on the shelf.

"Good," I respond with a smile.

"Maureen?" I look at her and she looks worried.

"Yes, mama?"

"I have to go away for three days on Monday. You're old enough now so I won't have someone watch you, but I hope you can be responsible."

My mama works from home, but occasionally she has to travel. The last time was about sixth months ago and I had to go stay with my grandma. My grandma is now in a nursing home so I can't go stay with her. That probably means that I'll be home alone which rarely ever happens. My mama trusts me, but she hates leaving me home alone.

My mama is usually only gone over the weekend or the beginning of the week. She doesn't like staying any longer than that. One time, she left on a Friday and had to stay until the next Thursday which made her angry. I don't what she does exactly, but I think she enjoys it. She's had this job since I was a little girl. I remember her leaving two or three times a year cause I would either get a babysitter or I would go stay with my grandma.

I've gotten used to it, but when I was young, I threw fits and begged her to stay. I got in trouble for it, but I always thought my mama was gonna leave me like my daddy. I know I shouldn't of thought like that, but I did and I cried every night until she returned. I've fortunately gotten over that. I stopped acting like that when I was nine years old and haven't been like that since.

"Okay. I think I can handle being on my own." I give her a reassuring smile.

"Hopefully. I trust you more now. You're going to be eighteen in a month so I expect you to be responsible enough." She smiles back then we walk back upstairs.

"Want me to help you cook?" It's an hour until six so I figure I should help make supper.

"No, go rest or something. I'll call you down around six." I nod before going upstairs.

I get in my room and leave the door open a bit. I then head for my bookshelf to pick out a book. I've read all of the books on my bookshelf, but there's room for more. I get a weekly allowance so I usually get a new book every week. The book that I pick out now is Stranger With My Face by Lois Duncan. She's one of my favorite authors.

I go over and sit on my window seat. I get lost in the book within minutes like I always do. I'm only on page one hundred and thirteen when I get called down to eat. I reluctantly mark my page and close my book then head downstairs. I go to the sink and wash my hands then sit down to eat.

"What were you doing up there? You were quiet." My mama questions.

"Reading." I answer as I get some food.

"Let me guess . . . a Lois Duncan book?" She grins.

"Yep." I smile back then hold out my hand. She grabs it gently then we say grace like we do before every meal.

"Maureen?" I look up at my mama.

"Yes?"

"There's been a change in plans . . I leave tomorrow morning. I have to leave the house by ten."

3.

I decide to get up early the next day and make my mama breakfast. I'm going to make her favorite, waffles and french toast with bacon. I see the time which is seven so I basically have two and a half hours. I get to work and move quickly, but carefully. After I get everything made, I go down to the basement to get a jar of strawberry jam.

I make toast and spread jam on it. I set the table with a satisfied grin on my face. I'm proud that I got this done in the amount of time I wanted to. As I finish setting the food on the table, I hear the wheels of a suitcase on the stairs.

"Maureen, did you do this for me?" I hear my mama exclaim from behind me.

"Of course I did," I reply as I turn to face her.

"Awe, you're so sweet. I love you so much." She pulls me into a hug.

"I love you, mama."

□*□*□*□

"I'll leave you money, use it wisely. You also have my cell number, the hotel number, my work number, my partner's number, correct?" My mama questions as we finish eating.

"Yes. You shouldn't worry. I can handle myself," I tell her as she stands up.

"Okay, okay. Give me a hug, Maureen." I get up and we hold each other for a while.

"You're gonna miss your flight." I pull away and I can tell she's on the verge of tears.

"Okay, I'm gonna leave before I start crying. I love you and I'll call you when I land."

"I love you more. Now go." I smile at her as she walks out the door.

I'm home alone now and I already feel the boredom creeping in. I go to the table and start cleaning up. I finish that then head upstairs. I go to my mama's room before going to mine. I decide that she'll probably have movies that aren't PG. I'm only allowed to watch PG movies and I can watch PG-13 with my mama. I look at a couple different movies then decide on the ones that are rated R.

I go to my room and put the first movie in my DVD player. I watch it and look away when they kiss or do more. I know now why my mama doesn't want me watching these kinds of movies. That doesn't stop me from watching the other ones even if I do feel awkward when watching them. I may be alone, but it still makes me feel uncomfortable.

I also get another feeling that I don't know how to describe. I ignore it and continue watching. I watch all of them then look at the clock to see that it's almost three-fifty. I just wasted half of my day watching movies in my pajamas. I instantly feel ashamed because I know my mama wouldn't ever let me do this unless I was sick.

I also didn't go to church because my mama said I didn't have to if I didn't want to. I obviously decided not to because I don't really enjoy church as much as I used to. My mama loves it and that's why her favorite day is Sunday. I go with her even though I don't enjoy it. It makes her happy when I go so I deal with it. She doesn't know that I don't enjoy it which is okay with me.

I change into overalls and a turquoise t-shirt. I put my hair in a ponytail after brushing it. I return the movies then go downstairs. I decide to clean a bit down here. I turn on the radio in the living room before I do anything. I change it from what my mama was listening to some pop music.

I start cleaning up the downstairs as I dance along to the music. I love when I can be like this. My mama would definitely disapprove of the music, saying how it's too sexual and suggestive. It may be that way to her, but it's fun to listen to or at least I think so. She prefers the channels that sing about God, faith, and stuff like that.

I continue humming along to the song as I sweep the foyer. I'm almost halfway done with the downstairs. I'll probably finish the rest tomorrow since it's almost five-thirty. I finish sweeping then put the broom away. I wash my hands then the phone starts ringing so I turn down the music before answering.

"Hello?" I ask as I fix my hair.

"Hi, honey. How is your day going?" I hear my mama ask.

"Good. I read a book then cleaned the downstairs." I lean against the wall, hoping she doesn't catch my lie.

"Oh, sounds like you were pretty productive." I know she's smiling.

"Yep, I figured that I should be useful. How was your flight?"

"Good, good. I landed about twenty minutes ago. I have a dinner in about an hour to discuss some things."

"Oh, maybe we should talk tomorrow so you have time to get ready?" I suggest.

"Probably. I love you."

"I love you." She hangs up after that and I sigh in relief.

I go to the kitchen to see what we have to eat. I decide on a ham sandwich and some chips. Before I make my sandwich, I turn the radio back up. I make it then sit at the table and eat. I finish eating my food then clean everything up. I turn off the radio and start to head upstairs when there's a knock at the door so I go to open it.

"Hey. Maureen, right?" It's the girl from yesterday.

I look at her outfit and wonder if this is how she always dresses. She's wearing a tank that has a monkey wearing a crown. Her jean shorts barely even reach the middle of her thighs. She's also barefoot even though it's kinda cold out.

"Yeah, why?" I reply.

"I'm Wednesday. I don't think we've actually met, but I think it's time we do." She smirks.

"You should come inside. It's cold out." I move aside and she steps inside. I shut the door.

"I like your place." She looks around.

"Thanks."

"But I like something a lot more." She looks at me with her another smirk.

"What's that?" I gulp when she steps closer.

"You."

4.

"What?" I ask as feelings of confusion and nervousness kick in.

Wednesday doesn't answer, but she does push me against a wall. She's eyeing me up and down with a look that I don't know how to describe. She pins my arms above my head and leans in so close that I can feel her breath on my face. I look her in the eyes and she's grinning. What's so funny about this?

"I'm going to do something and you might not like it at first," Wednesday tells me.

"Um okay."

Within seconds, her lips are against mine. I know it's wrong, but in that moment, I don't care what's right and what's wrong. I follow what she's doing which seems to be right. Her lips leave mine and she's kissing down my jawline then my neck. I'm about to pull away when she's does it for me.

"What would your mom think of this?" She jokes with a grin. She let's go of my arms.

"I don't know, but she doesn't have to know." I tell her and she looks surprised.

"What a naughty girl." She scolds, but I can tell she's joking.

"You're the one who kissed me." I defend myself, crossing my arms over my chest.

"But you kissed back, babygirl." She's so cocky and full of herself.

"You should get going." I squeeze past her to go open the door.

"Is that really what you want?" She raises an eyebrow.

"Yes." I lie.

"Keep telling yourself that, Maureen." She gives me a disapproving look before she walks out.

I shut the door behind her and lock it. I slide down after closing the door and sit on the floor. I can't believe that I just kissed Wednesday only moments ago. My mama would be so disappointed in me if she ever found out. She'd probably disown me if she knew how much I enjoyed it.

I couldn't help myself, though. It just felt so right when I was kissing Wednesday. I wonder if she feels the same way or was just kissing me for fun. I wish I could of talked to her more, but her teasing was getting on my nerves. She does live next door which means I could just go talk to her.

Before I know it, I'm walking upstairs to put on some shoes. I slip on my black flip-flops then head back downstairs. I look at myself in the mirror and decide that my hair needs redone. I do that quickly then walk out the door. I walk over to the Kinsley's house and knock on the door. The little boy answers.

"Hi, is Wednesday home?" I ask politely.

"Wednesday!" He yells and I jump.

"What?" Wednesday yells back from somewhere in the house.

"There's a girl here to see you!" It's silent for a couple minutes then I see her coming from the kitchen.

"Thanks, Cosmo. You can go bother someone else now." She smiles at him and he runs off.

"Hi, can we talk?" I bite my lip nervously when she doesn't answer right away.

"Sure, follow me." I do just that. We end up in the basement where her and Raphael's bedrooms are. I only know that because of the sign on one of the doors.

Her room takes up a whole side of the basement and Raphael's room takes up the other side. In between them is what appears to be a small living room type area. There's a sectional couch, two coffee tables, and a flat-screen T.V. along with a door on one side of the flat-screen. I follow her to her room which is on the right side. She shuts the door behind me then goes to sit on her bed.

"I'm guessing I freaked you the fuck out earlier. I'm sorry for that, but I had to kiss you." She explains as I take off my shoes. I then sit cross-legged beside her.

"You did freak me out. I've never kissed anyone before." I admit looking at her.

"That's obvious with the way your mom is . . . but it's also shocking." She looks at me.

"Why's that?"

"Cause you were the best fucking kiss that I've ever had and I've kissed a lot of people." I've never met someone who curses as much as Wednesday.

"I don't know what to say to that." I blush then look down.

"I do. I want to kiss you again and again. Maybe we could like keep thing a secret from your mom." I look up to see her grinning mischievously.

"Maybe. I'm still not sure about it." I'm trying to be as honest as possible.

"You should think about it cause I really enjoy being around you." She sits up.

"I'm not really sure how I feel." I tell her.

"I'll change your mind. I just know it." She smirks.

Wednesday crawls in my lap and attaches her lips to mine. I kiss back immediately because I love the way her lips feel on mine. I know I should want to pull away because this is a sin according to my mama, but I can't. Something must be wrong with me.

"I really enjoy kissing you." She smiles as she pulls away.

"I enjoy kissing you." I respond.

"Who wouldn't?" She's so confident and I'm not sure if I love it or hate it.

Before I can say anything else, she pecks my lips then gets up. I watch as she walks to the closet. I'm curious about what she's doing, but I stay seated on the bed. She appears a couple seconds later with something behind her bakc and a mischievous glint in her eyes. She comes back over to the bed, but the door opens and she shoves what appears to be a CD under her pillows.

"Hey, fuckface .. mom just fini-" Raphael stops suddenly when he sees me.

"I'll be up in a minute. Tell her to add another place at the table." Wednesday shoots him a glare, but he ignores it and nods.

"You want me to eat here?" I look at her and she nods.

"Of course I do." She smiles and gets up. I follow her back upstairs.

There's so much going on. The little siblings are hitting each other with pillows and laughing. Their daddy is talking to Raphael, but Raphael doesn't seem to care. Their mama is at the stove, pulling something out. Wednesday doesn't seem bothered by any of it because she walks towards the table as I follow behind.

I sit beside her at the table. There's a long bench on side that curves. It looks to be something out of a diner. There's also chairs that don't match it at all. The chairs are all a different, outrageous color or design. My chair is neon orange with a hot pink seat cushion while Wednesday's is bright purple with a neon yellow cushion.

"Everybody at the table. The food is done," Their mama yells over the noise.

"What is it?" The little girl asks as she runs to the table.

"Pizza casserole, Velma," Her mama responds with a proud grin.

"Yay! That's my favorite!" Cosmo shouts with a grin.

"Mine, too." His daddy grins as he sits down. The children and Raphael sit on the long side of the bench while their daddy sits on the corner with their mama.

"Wait, you're that neighbor girl. Maureen, right?" Their daddy looks at me causing all eyes to suddenly be on me.

"Yes, sir." I respond. Their mama starts dishing out food. After everybody's plates have food on them, she puts the tray in the middle of the table.

"Call me, Dale. My wife's name is Shaina. I'm guessing you know every-body else's names."

"Yep."

"It's nice to meet you. Wednesday doesn't bring much of her friends around here. I hope Velma doesn't do that. I love meeting new people." Their mama explains to me with a grin.

"So . . Wednesday, are you and Maureen in a relationship?" Raphael asks smirking.

"Nope, just friends. Not every girl I bring home is my girlfriend." Wednes-day glares at him and he glares right back.

"Are you staying the night?" Velma asks.

"I don't think so. I've never been away from home before. My mama also doesn't know I'm here." I explain to the little girl.

"Maybe I could stay at your place? You're gonna be alone so I could keep you company." Wednesday sounds hopeful.

"I guess so. I've never been home alone before. My mama can't know, though. She'd be extremely mad that I had you over without permission."

"We won't tell if you won't." Their mama says with a wink.

"Okie dokie. I guess it'd be nice to have some company." I smile at their mama then we continue eating.

□*□*□*□

"So . . this is your room?" Wednesday asks as she looks around my room.

"Yep, it sure is," I reply with a proud grin.

"I like it." She sets her bag on my desk chair.

"Thanks."

"I know something fun we can do." She looks at me and I sense mischievousness.

"Uhm . .what?" I'm unsure of what she's up to.

"Talk, I don't really know you." She walks over to my bookshelf with a grin on her face.

"Oh . . okay." I'm relieved by that because I thought she was gonna say something worse.

"I'm going to guess this is one of your favorite books." She holds up, Wherever Nina Lies by Lynn Weingarten.

"One of them." I grin, but that disappears when her hand touches the top shelf.

"Does your mom know about this?" She asks me a minute later.

I have books that I know my mom wouldn't approve of. I hide them behind other books on the top shelf so she doesn't know. Wednesday figures that out and is now looking through the books. I'm okay with her knowing I guess.

"Chosen sounds like an interesting book." She's looking through, Chosen by Barbara Elsborg which is honestly one of my favorite books.

"It is. You can borrow it if you want." She looks surprised, but keeps the book in her hand.

"Beneath The Burn sounds interesting also." Beneath The Burn is by Pam Godwin and I think she did a good job writing it.

"You can borrow that one, too." She smiles then walks over to her bag. She puts the books in her bag.

"What movies do you have?" She moves her bag to the floor then sits in the chair.

"Uhm, mainly Disney and similar stuff to that." I reply as I sit on my bed.

"What about any action movies or horror movies?" I shake my head.

"I'm not allowed to watch them."

"Damn, I'll call Raphael. He'll bring some over." She pulls out her cell then calls Raphael.

"Hey, Raph. Can you do something for me?" She asks in a hopeful tone as she puts it on speaker.

"Depends on what it is." I can tell he's smirking.

"Get a couple movies for us. Like my Nightmare On Elm Street series and my Scream series."

"Yeah, sure. Where are they?" I hear shuffling around then a door open. I hear another door opening.

"Uhm, try the top shelf of my closet." I hear the squeaking of her closet doors then more shuffling.

"Got them. I'll be over in fivish." He hangs up after that so I start to head downstairs.

"Are those horror movies?" I ask her as we reach the second floor.

"Yep, two of my favorites." She grins proudly.

"Open up bitches! I'm here!" Raphael yells as he pounds on the door.

"Coming!" Wednesday yells as she rushes down the stairs. She opens the door and he's leaning against the doorway with a smug look.

"Hello ladies. Am I allowed in?" He smirks.

"Yes." I respond as Wednesday says no.

"Can I stay?"

"Sure." Wednesday glares at me, but I shrug it off.

5.

"**O**MG, no!" I shriek covering my eyes.

"Dude, he just threw him over a balcony. That ain't that bad." Raphael tells me with a smile as he grabs a handful of popcorn.

"Yes, it is. Why would someone do that?" I reply, defending myself.

"Ladies, be quiet when someone dies. It's disrespectful to talk," Wednesday jokes.

"You two are terrible." I shake my head, but continue to watch.

"Yes, yes we are." Raphael looks at me with a creepy look then goes back to watching the movie.

We continue watching the movie with me jumping and screaming occasionally. After this one, we watch the fourth Scream. I'm thankful that it's the last movie in this series. They may be good movies, but they're gory and kinda scary. I could watch them again, but I'd probably still look away at certain parts.

Nightmare On Elm Street is after these. It's almost one in the morning by this point. We'll probably be up all night just to finish the movies. I'm not even tired and I don't think Raphael or Wednesday are tired either. It doesn't help that they made coffee and put lots of sugar in it, too.

"So what did you think of the Scream series?" Wednesday asks as the fourth one ends.

"They're good. Gruesome, but good," I reply with a smile.

"We'll, we're not even done with this marathon at least not yet." Raphael gets up then puts in the next movie.

□*□*□*□

"I'm exhausted," I say with a yawn.

"At least we finished them. Now we can sleep," Wednesday tells me while she stretches.

"I like sleeping. Especially on this comfy couch," Raphael says in a sleepy voice.

"You can stay I guess. We can sleep on the bed." I get up and so does Wednesday.

"I have to pee." She heads towards the bathroom.

"Wait, me too." I follow her in the bathroom then close the door. I look away before she gets to the toilet.

"I'm glad we could do this. It's been really fun." I hear her flush then I turn around to see her walking to the sink.

"Yeah, it has." I use the toilet then I wash my hands. We walk out as Raphael sets his phone down.

"I need a bigger blanket." He looks at us.

"Hold on." I walk to my closet and grab a blanket off the top shelf. I walk back out and hand it to him.

"My favorite color and design." He jokes with a smile.

"Oh, c'mon . . who doesn't like a hot pink blanket with purple hearts and turquoise butterflies." She tells him with a grin. I'm about to say something when the phone goes off so I walk over to my night stand.

"Hello," I say.

"Hi, Maureen. How's it going?" My mom replies.

"Good, I'm working on cleaning up my room right now." I lie.

"That's nice. I'm glad you're being responsible." I can tell she's smiling.

"Yeah, I think might make lunch after I finish." I lie again.

"Thanks, I really appreciate all this. You're doing great with being alone."

"Welcome, it's not even that big of a deal." I look at Wednesday and Raphael who are both watching me.

"I raised such a good daughter. I'm proud of you, Maureen."

"I know you are. You tell me that a lot." I smile.

"Because it's true. Anyways I have a meeting to go to so I'll talk to you later, okay?"

"Okay, bye. Love you."

"I love you, too." With that, she hangs up.

"Now we can sleep." I smile then lay on the bed and close my eyes.

I fall asleep quickly and groan when someone starts trying to wake me up. I ignore them and continue trying to sleep.

"MAUREEN!" Someone shouts. I jump up and look to see Wednesday with a satisfied look on her face.

"Was that really necessary?" I ask while I glare at her.

"Yes cause it woke you up," Raphael says. I look to see him at my desk.

"What are you doing?" I look as he continues spinning in the chair.

"Waiting for you to get up." Wednesday stands up then goes to my closet.

"Why?"

"Cause we're going somewhere. All of us." Raphael stops spinning then looks around the room with a goofy grin.

"Here, wear this. I like it." Wednesday throws clothes at me and I shoot a glare at her and she smiles.

"I'll be back." I get up and go to my bathroom.

I look at the clothes that she picked out and roll my eyes. It's something my mom hates, but doesn't want me to get rid of it. My aunt got it for me a year ago for my birthday. She said she got it cause I don't have any clothes that a seventeen year old girl should wear. I like it, but I'm only allowed to wear it when I'm with my aunt.

It's a pale pink shirt that's low-cut and has staps. The shirt also only reaches just above my belly button. I have to wear a strapless bra with it and I guess Wednesday figured that out. The skirt that goes with it barely reaches my thighs. I always wear a leather jacket with it so I'll have to grab that. I look at the underwear and gasp, but put it on anyways.

"Damn, Maureen." Raphael looks at me with a smirk and I blush.

"Back off, she's mine." Wednesday gives him a dirty look.

"She's not a couch, ya know?" Raphael tells her matter of factly.

"Oh, shut it." She rolls her eyes as I pick out a pair of shoes. I go with my black flip-flops then I grab my leather jacket.

"Ready?" I ask.

"You should do something with her hair. Make her look extra pretty." Raphael tells Wednesday.

"You actually said something smart for once. Wow, good job." She fakes being shocked then leads me to the bathroom. I sit down and she starts doing something with my hair, but she won't let me look.

"Are you done?" I ask when her hands aren't messing with my hair.

"I think so. Here, look." I look and smile.

"I love it." My hair is in somewhat of a side bun, but with braid around it.

"Good, I worked hard." I stand up and we walk out.

"You two look like a couple, a cute lesbian couple that everybody is jealous of."

"Was that supposed to be a compliment or you being an ass?" Wednesday looks at him.

"Compliment, now let's go." He quickly gets up then opens my door dramatically.

"Gosh, he's weird." I shake my head, trying to smile.

"It runs in the family." She grabs my hand and we head downstairs. I immediately want to run back upstairs when I see who's down there.

6.

"Maureen Judith Baker!" The person calls after me. I continue running up the stairs.

"Is that your mom?" Wednesday asks as she follows me.

"I'll tell you in a minute." I respond.

"I'm not gonna tell your mom! I'm your cool aunt who let's you get away with anything and everything!" I stop and then turn around.

"Aunt Annette, as much as I love and trust you . . I know my mother sent you here to spy on me." I look at her.

"She did, but that literally means nothing. I came here to check up on you and then lie to your mother about what you're doing." She grins.

"Is that the truth?" I'm still skeptical, but Annette is pretty relaxed and carefree.

"Yes, now introduce me to your friends, but in the kitchen cause I'm hungry." She starts walking back downstairs and I realize something.

"OMG are you pregnant?" I shout as I rush back downstairs.

"How'd you know? I mean, no." Annette face palms and I smile.

"Who's the daddy?" I jump up bad sit on the counter.

"Uhm, Carlos or maybe Isaac or Dylan. No, his name was Mark. Actually, I don't know. He was hot like really hot and I couldn't help myself. He also had a lot of tattoos then there was the piercings and next thing I know . . I'm pregnant." She shrugs then starts going through the fridge.

"Don't tell grandma that. You'd be in trouble." I joke.

"If my mom saw him, she would be cured of everything, I swear." She pulls out the pickles and starts eating them.

"Wow, that's intense. He must of been really good looking." I look at her and she nods.

"You don't even know. I wish I got his number, but his girlfriend was knocking on the door at like ten in the morning so I had to go out the bathroom window. I left my favorite bra there on purpose so maybe the girlfriend would see it." She pauses, "Wow, I'm such a bitch." She adds on.

"I love your aunt." Wednesday smiles.

"Who doesn't? I'm such an awesome person. Anyways, is this your girl-friend?" Annette looks at Wednesday.

"I wish, but her mom is kinda preventing that."

"Ooohh, been there. Did you know your mom scared away my first girl-friend?" Annette looks at me with a serious look.

"Really?"

"Yep, I was almost eighteen so I was already breaking rules. Her name was Lana. I fell for her and one night, I snuck out. She stopped me then made me decide between a home and Lana."

"What about Granny? Where was she?"

"Off with your Gramps on some vacation in Greece. Laurel was older so she was in charge of me."

"She would of been like twenty-six."

"Yep, I haven't talked to Lana since. I heard from someone that she's a pornstar."

"A what?" I'm confused.

"You'll find out someday." Raphael speaks up from the other side of the kitchen.

"Were y'all going somewhere?" Annette puts the pickles away.

"Yeah, Maureen needs to experience normal teen life."

"Yes, she does. You guys go have fun. I'll be here eating."

□*□*□*□

"I could never wear something like that!" I exclaim as Wednesday holds up a lacy bra.

"Yes, you could. You'd look hot in it. Just try it on." Wednesday begs.

"Fine." I grab it since it's my size then go to the dressing rooms.

I take off my jacket then my shirt. I remove my bra then put the lacy one on. I look at in the mirror for a couple seconds then I decide that I will keep it. I put my clothes back on them walk back out.

"I like it." I tell her and grins proudly.

"Let's find more clothes and stuff."

We do just that and end up spending way more than I would have liked. Wednesday and Raphael keep reminding me that it's okay, but I feel bad. They wouldn't even let me pay for anything which also meant I couldn't see the final price of anything. I know I'll have to hide most of it from my mama.

"Stop pouting. If we couldn't of afforded the clothes and other things, we wouldn't of bought it." Raphael tells me while glancing through the rearview mirror.

"And besides, this is what friends do. We're friends, right?" Wednesday turns around to look at me.

"I think so. I've never really had friends before." I truthfully tell her.

"Well you do now." Raphael smiles and I smile back. Friends, such a weird concept to think about.

My mama would definitely be angry about who I made friends with, but it's really not her choice. Teenagers need friends, not just their parents. I have my mom for support, but I can't tell her everything. I have secrets, secrets that I sometimes want to talk about, but not with my mom. This is one of those secrets and I know I could never tell her.

At least I have, Annette. I think she understands me more than my mom. She's like me in a way and I connect more with her than my mama. She was like me at one point, young and curious. She's always doing stuff for me without me even asking.

Sometimes, I wish my mama was like her, but that's only a wish . . a wish that would never come true. My mama is religious and strict unlike Annette. Annette is somewhat of an atheist and laid back. She's never yelled at me even when I've probably deserved it. My mama always seems to be yelling.

"We're home!" Wednesday exclaims as we pull in my drive.

"You scream way too fucking much." Raphael glare at her.

"That's not what your girlfriend was saying." Wednesday smirks before getting out of the car. I get out next.

"I don't even have a girlfriend! I have a boyfriend!" He shouts as she runs up to my house with bags.

"Maureen?" I turn around to see Ms. Striplin.

"Oh, hi." I smile and she looks at Raphael.

"Who's this?" She gives him a skeptical look. I already know she knows who he is. I also know she's gonna tell my mama.

"I had her invite him over. Maureen has only a few friends so I thought neighbors would be a good start," Annette says from behind me. I mentally sigh in relief.

"Does her mother know?"

"Not yet. I was planning on telling her when she calls later." I can hear the annoyance in Annette's voice.

"Oh, well y'all have a nice day." She smiles before walking away.

"Yeah, whatever . . Ms. Nosylin." I see Annette roll her eyes. She grabs a couple bags then we all head inside.

"What was that nosy bitch doing here?" Wednesday asks as she comes from the kitchen with a popsicle. We just set the bags down.

"Being nosy." Raphael replies.

"Ah, of course. I hate her." Wednesday's green eyes show a hint of anger for a second.

"Me too." I reply.

"At least she didn't call you a slut on your thirteenth birthday for wearing a bikini top and shorts in front of your house." Wednesday exaggerates the word your.

"Damn, she needs to mind her own business." Annette shakes her head.

"She doesn't know how." Raphael smiles.

"Obviously. Who's hungry? I'm good at making peanut butter and jelly sandwiches."

"We could just order food." I suggest.

"Good thinking." The phone starts ringing.

"You should get that." I look at Annette and she nods.

"Hi, this is the best person to ever exist. How may I be of service to you on this fine evening?" Annette puts the phone on speaker.

"Annette, are those kids still there?" I hear my mom ask.

"Of course, Laurie. Maureen needs friends."

"My name's Laurel, not Laurie. Stop acting childish. Get rid of them."

"They are teenagers, not rats." Annette tells her defending Raphael and Wednesday.

"Teenagers don't act like they do. Their parents should've raised them better." I hear the disgust in my mama's voice and it angers me.

"At least they're happy. I wasn't happy at all with the way mom raised us." I watch as Annette gets angrier.

"Mom raised us just fine. You had everything you needed, but you still acted out. You were the reason for all her stress."

"I had everything, but not freedom. I had no freedom in that household."

"Bullshit! I turned out just fine and I was treated the exact same way as you." My mama only curses when she's really angry.

"We were so not treated the same way. Mom loved you more than me. It was obvious to everyone. Why do you think Aunt Sunny treated me better than you?"

"Because you two are similar, young and reckless. I'm surprised you aren't pregnant, yet. Aunt Sunny was pregnant at the age of nineteen and she didn't even know who the father was. That's why Raina acted the way she did."

"Raina didn't act any specific way. If anything, she was shy and quiet. Barely ever spoke. And weren't you pregnant at the age of twenty-two with some guy you met at a party?" Wednesday mutters roasted under her breath and Raphael smiles.

"At least I raised my child properly. Maureen doesn't act out and she's a good girl unlike Raina. Raina ended up running away at eighteen and nobody has seen her since."

"How do you know Maureen is such a good girl? You know nothing about children."

"Because she's my daughter."

"Yeah, I know. She's such an unlucky child. I don't know why she hasn't run off yet." Annette smiles.

"You little bitch! I want you out of my house before I get back or I am calling the police on you!" With that, my mama hangs up.

"I definitely won that."

7.

"Get up! I made breakfast and I want y'all to try it before I do in case I messed up!" Annette shouts the next morning.

"Did someone mention food?" Raphael bolts up from the couch.

"Yep." He gets up quickly and I notice he isn't wearing a shirt, possibly no pants either.

"I like food, too," Wednesday mumbles.

"Good. Be downstairs in ten minutes. Also get dressed, I'm taking you somewhere." Annette smirks before leaving.

"I love your aunt. I also love your house." Raphael glances at me before grabbing his book bag.

"I agree with you for once, Raph." Wednesday gets up at the same I do.

"Thanks, I think," I respond going in my closet.

"Wear something new!" Wednesday exclaims.

I look through the new stuff. I think it was supposed to be nice out today. I pick out a white halter top and jean shorts along with some heeled ankle boots. I walk out and see Wednesday waiting for me.

"Finally." She walks to the bathroom and holds the door open for me. I walk on after and lock the door.

"Will this look okay? I've never worn clothes like this before."

"Of course. Now let me pee in peace."

□*□*□*□

"Where are we going?" I ask as we get in Annette's car.

"A tour of my teenage life," Annette responds.

"This sounds fun," Raphael says from the front seat.

"Where should we stop first . . my first kiss or where I met the guy who took my virginity?"

"First kiss then where you met the guy who took your virginity so you can then show us how romantic the place where you lost it was." Wednesday explains.

"Good thinking, Wednesday."

"She's not usually this smart." Raphael jokes.

"Shut up. I'm not the one who dropped out of college."

"At least I got accepted into college."

"Yeah, but only cause you flirted your way in."

"It worked, didn't it?" Raph smirks.

"Yeah and now you're dating him."

"Actually I'm not. We broke up last night cause he's moving to London so he can meet a British guy. British people are supposedly sexier."

"They are." Wednesday smiles.

"Shut up. I already know that."

"We're here." Annette interjects.

I look and we're a rundown park. The swingset is partly in the ground and the slide leads into a huge puddle of mud. The playset thingy is falling apart and half of it has already fallen off. There's not even anybody around.

"It's always been like this, but when I was fourteen, it was a bit better." Annette gets out and we follow her to the swingset.

"Is it even safe to sit here?" I ask.

"Probably not, but it makes the story more realistic."

"I'm not sitting." Wednesday leans against the poles.

"I am." Raph sits down while I stand there.

"Okay, let's get started." Annette pauses then starts again, "Imagine a cold May night, now add me and a boy who was way too old to be with a fourteen year old." She looks at us.

"How old?" Raph asks.

"Twenty-one."

"Got it." Wednesday nods.

"Okay, that night I snuck out to meet him even though we only ever emailed each other. We didn't know what each other looked like, but we knew the ages of the other. He brought alcohol and I brought nothing, but myself. We talked for a couple minutes then started drinking, I don't even remember what it was, but I got a major hangover. I remember his lips, though and how his mouth felt against mine . . he was perfect."

"After the kiss, he smiled and told me that I was one of his best kisses. I knew he was telling the truth because he kissed me again and again. After all those kisses and hands all over me, he never emailed me again. This happened right here on this swing and I come back here sometimes to remember it even though it makes me want him back."

"Damn, that's book worthy." Wednesday looks at her.

"I know, but I'm not the greatest when it comes to writing." Annette sits there for a couple more seconds then gets up.

"Where to next?" We all get in the car.

"It's like five minutes away." She's right and within five minutes we're at a gas station that I don't even recognize.

"Where is this?" Raphael looks around.

"Where I met the guy who changed my life, but not in a good way."

"Explain, please." Wednesday looks at my aunt.

"Okay so . . he worked here and he wasn't what you imagined. His name is Frank, by the way. It was almost like a young adult romance novel in real life. He was super hot like I couldn't even think when I was near him. I always came here after the first time I saw him, but this time was different. Keep in mind, I was sixteen and clueless as to what real love actually was."

"Anyways, I came in here one day in my best outfit that I could put together without looking desperate. It was shorts that were probably too short and a tank top with a floral design that showed off enough. I saw Frank looking at me the whole time, but he didn't know I saw him looking at me. I purposely bent down in front of him then when I got everything I needed, I left. He chased after me, though and I was proud of myself."

"We went on two dates after this which were so romantic and nice like I was so happy. The happiest that I had been in a while. Frank was a sweet guy, too except that he was nineteen and he had asshole friends. I dealt with his friends by acting disinterested and showing them that I was in love with their friend, not them."

"We went way too fast in our relationship. Frank didn't pressure me, though. I was trying to act older so he would like me more. That takes us to the next stop." She starts driving again and we end up at a house not too far from the gas station.

"This was Frank's house, usually always empty because his dad was never home. His dad was always travelling or at least that's what his dad told him. Anyways, I was here one night with and his friends hanging out in the basement like we always did. It was a relaxed night and we were all getting along without any mean comments. One of Frank's friends kept asking questions about our relationship which wasn't any of his business."

"This guy had the nerve to ask if I was still virgin then proceeded to tell me that most of Frank's girls don't make it past the third month. Frank glared at him and the guy just laughed and looked at me with the strangest look ever like he wanted something. I felt uncomfortable and I looked at Frank who was seething. I watched as one of his friends stood up then another. I watched Frank's lips mouth, run which I ignored until I had a clear path."

"Another guy stood up and this was when I took the opportunity to run. I almost made it to the top when I was grabbed and dragged back to the couch. I was screaming, but not crying while Frank was trying to break free of his friends' hold on him. I knew I was in trouble and that I was about to in the worst situation that I've ever been in until Frank said something. He told him that he'd do it and I was thankful in a way."

"Frank's friends liked that idea better and I did, too. I didn't want to lose my virginity that way, but I did. After that, nothing was the same between us and the spark was gone. He broke up with me and we never spoke again because we didn't want to be reminded of what he had to do. He sent a letter to me a year after everything."

"Here, I'll show you guys." I watch as she pulls an envelope from the glove compartment.

"I don't want to read that. I think I'll cry." Raph tells her.

"Same here."

"I will." My aunt hands me the envelope.

It's worn and faded like it has been read more than once. I open it carefully and take the letter out.

My dearest Annie,   I'm still sorry for what happened even if it has been a year. I regret it every single day and I wish it never happened because I truly did love you. I still imagine a future for us, one without my friends, one without your mom and sister, one where it's just us. Sometimes I actually believe it, isn't that funny? I bet you've forgotten me or have blocked out any image of us which is probably best. I basically took advantage of you and it still haunts me because I could of tried harder, I should of. God, I should of fought them off or got you out of there. I had my eyes closed the whole time and it was only because I couldn't see my girl hurt. I've cried every night since and I know you probably have, too. I can't believe what I put you through. You were only sixteen and I did that to you, how will you ever recover? The saddest day of my life was saying goodbye to you because I thought I was going to spend the rest of my life with you. I don't think I could bear it if I didn't say that I'm still sorry before I left. You're not mine to love anymore, but I still love you, Annie. I love you, but it's too late for us. I see you sometimes and all I can think of is how much I miss you. I'm a mess without you and I don't know what to do. This letter is probably a mess, too. I'm sorry if it makes no sense, but I just wanted to apologize one last time, I wanted to tell you that I still love you, and that I miss you. Now it's time for goodbye because I'm going away and one day we'll meet again, it'll be better this way, I promise.   Love,   Frank

"He killed himself, didn't he?"

"Yeah . . he did and I almost did, too."

8.

- -

"He really loved you," Wednesday says.

"Yeah, he'd probably still be alive if it weren't for his friends. I know it's not right to blame them, but I do. I will always will blame them," Annette says with a hint of sadness.

"I can't even imagine how someone could do that," Raph says.

"You're not the only one." Annette starts the car.

"Where we going next?" I ask.

"Where I met the guy who I thought could help me, fix me even." We end up at the library.

"This isn't our only stop, is it?" Raph looks at her and she shakes her head.

"I got a job here a week after my seventeenth birthday. His name was Jerome which I learned after the third time he came in. I was still getting over Frank so I wasn't interested at first, but he was persistent. One day I gave in and his whole face lit up like it was the best day of his life. I felt like he was the one who could help me in that moment."

"The next Friday, he took me on a date to this fancy place. I felt special and loved, it almost felt like he actually wanted to be with me. The date was nice until the end of it. He wanted to go to a party which I wasn't okay with. I feared that I'd somehow see Frank's friends there. That should of been the least of my worries because Jerome had a plan set up for me that I wasn't aware of." We end up at a house with a for sale sign in the yard.

"I stayed close to him the whole time we were there which probably made him think that I actually enjoyed being around him. I was scared, but he must not of seen that and if he did . . he ignored it. I waited for an hour and a half before trying to get him to leave. I made up excuses and told him lies to try and get him to leave. He got angry and took me upstairs to a bedroom which made me panic."

"Jerome's grip on my arm was too tight and I couldn't even get him to let go. My vision started to get blurry and breathing felt impossible. I felt like I was going to die and he didn't even notice. I tried screaming, but all I could do was gasp and cry. Luckily, someone saved me and got Jerome away. She was my hero and my second love."

"Lana." Wednesday looks at Annette who just nods.

"We have three stops now." She starts driving and we end up at a house that's falling apart.

"This is where I stayed the night of the party because I had nowhere to go since I told Granny I was staying at a friends. Lana lived here with her two sisters, two brothers, three dogs, five cats, and her parents. It was always crowded, but she didn't have to share a room so we had a bit of privacy. Her room was in the attic along with her older brother's room. There was only four rooms, not including the two in the attic."

"Anyways, we got home that night and we had to sneak through the second story bathroom window. Luckily, it was like eleven by the time we got to

Lana's house so not many people were up. We snuck back up to the attic and into her room where she let me change into some of her clothes. She didn't make me talk about anything and she let me stay til most of the next day. I went home and kept what happened a secret."

"Next stop is granny's old house, isn't it?" I look at her and she nods. We head to there. My mom said that granny lived here until I was three.

"The next weekend was the best weekend ever. Lana came over on Friday and stayed until Sunday which pissed your mom off. Granny was happy for me, though. Lana and I stayed in my room most of the weekend. Saturday night was the best night ever cause we kissed, and it wasn't just once."

"We started dating after that, knowing that it was the right thing to do. Lana brought happiness into my life, but that wasn't the only thing she brought. I experienced many new things because of her, but I also got in trouble. Granny started to despise her, the good thing is that she didn't know we dating. She would of flipped if she knew what we did under her roof."

"Your mom ruined the whole relationship after a year. She caught us making out in nothing, but our underwear. Our clothes were scattered all over my floor and that's the second thing that your mom noticed. She called Granny immediately and told her what she saw. Lana was thrown out after we got dressed, but that didn't stop us."

"We met in secret and continued being together until I got caught sneaking out. Your mom came over and I thought I could trick her, but I was wrong. I was only in a bikini top and short shorts cause Lana and I were going to go skinny dipping in the city pool. I didn't mention Lana once, but that's what they assumed, that I was going to see her. I got grounded and they put bars on my windows so I wouldn't sneak out again."

"I did find a way out and that's where our last stop is." We end up at train station that's about forty minutes away.

"This is where I last saw Lana. We kissed one last time then she left. I never have saw her again."

"Why'd she have to leave?" Wednesday asks.

"Granny convinced her parents to send her to some family in Ireland. She had to get on the train so she could go see to her grandparents who would then send her to Ireland."

"Wow, that's just terrible." Raph tells my aunt.

"Yeah, it sure is."

"Mama should of just minded her own business. You were happy, why would she want to take that away?"

"Your mama is a selfish woman."

"Sometimes I think she is, too." I admit.

"Let's head back."

We head back and all I can do is think. My mama is so small minded and I guess that's a side effect of living in a small town. Small towns aren't anything like in books. They're full of people who judge you and try to make you believe things that aren't true. I've never been judged, but I've seen people do it. My mama does it a lot and it angers me.

I've never known anything from what my mama has told me. I've somehow managed to not be as judgemental as her. I accept people the way they are without judging them. I don't care how people act or what they look like. I think you should be allowed to look however you want and act however you want as long as you're kind to others.

"C'mon, I'll order food since it's like four." We get out and without think-ing, I grab ahold of Wednesday's hand.

"Finally. I've been wanting to do that all day." She smiles sheepishly.

We all walk in the house together. Annette gets food for all of us then we sit around the table and talk. We get to know each other and it honestly makes me happy. This day has been amazing to me even if it was a bit sad.

□*□*□*□

We wake up to knocking on the door. Annette yells that she'll get it so inlay back down. I almost fall back asleep when I hear my mama call my name.

9.

"Yes, mama?" I ask when I get downstairs. I'm holding Wednesday's hand.

"What do you think you're doing?" She asks glaring at Wednesday.

"What does it look like I'm doing?" I suddenly feel angry at how she's treating Wednesday.

"You are acting up. I will not tolerate this, young lady." She stomps towards us and pulls us apart which causes me to crash to the floor.

"Laurel!" Annette yells.

"You did this!" She gestures between Wednesday and I, "You caused my daughter to be one of them!" My mama is yelling.

"There is nothing wrong with being a lesbian! Your daughter is still your daughter even if she prefers girls!" Annette yells defending me.

"No, she isn't. No daughter of mine will date girls, let alone kiss them!"

"You will not do that to her. She won't end up like me. She'll continue being with the girl who she likes! It won't be like Lana and I!" Annette gives my mama a hateful look.

"Lana was the reason you were like that! She caused it!"

"No, she didn't because I kissed her first and I told her that I loved her first! I lost the love of my life because you and mom are so small minded!"

"Don't talk about mom like that! You should know better than to speak ill of her. She's dying for goodness sakes!"

"You can't tell me what to do anymore. I'm twenty-two for God sakes! You can't treat me like a child anymore!"

"I wouldn't have to, but you still act like one!"

"Well, this child is fucking pregnant and you will never see my baby!"

"You don't even know who the father is. You probably met him at a bar them went home with him!"

"So what if I did? That doesn't make my baby any less important!"

"Your child is a mistake and you know it!" I watch as Annette punches my mama in the face then as my mama falls to the ground.

"You just knocked her out," Raph mutters.

"I sure did. You guys go home and Maureen go pack a bag."

"I'll go up with you to get our stuff." Wednesday follows behind me.

"I'm sorry you had to see that." I tell Wednesday as I shut the door behind us.

"Just kiss me, Maureen." I nod before I attach my lips to hers. I don't want to pull away, but I force myself to. Wednesday gives me a questioning look.

"I think I'm in love with you, but I have no idea what to do." I admit.

"Me too. Maybe we'll just see what happens."

"I like that idea."

"I like you." She grins as I walk in my closet. I grab my suitcase then the duffle bag that goes with it.

"Can you help?"

"Let me text Raph." She does then starts helping.

I pack my favorite books in a bookbag first because those are the most important to me. While I do that, Wednesday packs as much clothes that she can fit in the suitcase and duffle bag. I grab the necessary toiletries, but don't include any of my shower stuff then put those in the duffle bag. I grab my journal that's underneath my desk surface then head downstairs.

"Where's my mama?" I ask Annette.

"Raph helped me carry her to he room. He's at home by the way." Annette smiles at Wednesday.

"Okay, well I'll see you guys later." She leaves them I look at Annette.

"You're gonna stay at my place for a while. First, we have to stop somewhere." I nod then follow Annette to her car. We put my things in the trunk.

"Where's this stop?" I look at her as she starts the car.

"Don't worry about it, okay?" She glances at me and I nod.

□*□*□*□

"You're going to try and adopt me?!" I exclaim.

"I'm pretty sure that's why I got the adoption papers," Annette replies. It's currently almost three in the afternoon.

"My mama would never let that happen. You're going to have to go to court."

"I know, but it's all for you. It's to make you happier." She grins at me.

"Thank you for this, Annette." I grin back.

"It's no problem. Your mama is at fault here."

"I know." We get in her car then head back to her house.

Annette used the money from Granny to get a decent sized house(Granny gave her money to get her out of the house). It's a three story house with a gate surrounding the property. She has a pool in the back along with a flower garden. I have my own room when I come here since she has six bedrooms.

The third floor is my favorite part of the house. It's just a huge room with a home theater, a few arcade games, and a small kitchen. Annette spent most of her money on the third floor. My mama doesn't really know about it, she just thinks it's the attic since that's what it originally was. Annette and I usually hang out up there.

When we get to the house, I head up to my room. I set my stuff on the floor then lay on the bed. Today has been the most stressful day that I've had in a long time. I can't believe Annette actually wants to adopt me. She already has a baby on the way so it's pretty weird to me.

Maybe Annette just needs help or wants me around to clean. I doubt she'd ever do that, though. My mama would definitely do that to someone, but Annette probably wouldn't. Annette has always been nicer to me than my mama which sounds weird. It's sad to think like that or at least it is me.

Your parents shouldn't be allowed to be mean to you and it's a terrible thing when it happens.

"Maureen?" I look to see my aunt.

"Yes, Annette?" I reply.

"I'm going to talk to your mom. If you want to call Wednesday and invite her over . . you can." She smiles, but I can tell she's upset.

"Okay, do you have her number?"

"It's on a piece of paper by the phone." She stands there for a couple more seconds then starts.

"Annette," She stops and turns around, "Are you okay?"

"I'll be fine, honey. Don't worry about me, okay?" She doesn't let me respond because she's already closing my door.

I wait until she leaves to go downstairs. I walk to the area where her phone is and I see a number. I hesitate for a couple seconds before dialing the number. After a couple rings, Wednesday answers.

"Uh, hello?" I hear her voice and instantly grin.

"Hey, it's Maureen. What are you doing right now?" I ask.

"Wishing that I was with you, why do you ask?" I can hear the grin in her voice.

"Cause I was wishing the same thing. Can you come over to Annette's house if I give you the address?" I bite my lip within seconds of asking.

"Possibly. What's the address?"

I then tell her the address. She then puts my on hold to go ask her mom. When I say on hold, I mean she turns on some music while she runs upstairs. I wait nervously which is weird to me since I'm usually never this nervous.

"She said yes. I'll be there in about twenty minutes. Bye, baby girl." She hangs up and I squeal like a little girl.

I run upstairs and fix my hair. I then check my outfit which Wednesday helped pick out. She insists on me wearing my new clothes because they make me look way cuter. I can't help, but agree with her which may sound vain or something like that. In my opinion, it's completely stupid that I can't think that I look good without people calling me vain or full of myself.

I start unpacking while I wait. I unpack my clothes first and put those in the closet. I already have clothes in here cause Annette bought me some. She's always doing stuff like that, but I sometimes feel guilty when she does it. She insists that it's okay, but it still makes me feel guilty.

I don't unpack my books just yet. I'll save that for when I officially know I'm staying here. I know that sounds strange, but it makes sense to me. I know my mama will fight this whole situation. Half of me wants my mama to win, but the other half wants Annette to win. My thoughts are interrupted by a loud knock on the front door.

"Coming!" I shout as I quickly make my way downstairs.

"Raph isn't with me so it'll be just us," Wednesday tells me and I almost smile. It'll finally just be us.

"Oh okay. Well come in." I move out of the way and she immediately looks around.

"Is this really Annette's house? I always imagined her in a small apartment or something like that."

"Yeah, it's what she spent a lot of the money my Granny gave her on."

"That's smart of her."

"Yeah, let's go upstairs so you can set your bag down." She follows me to my room.

"Whoa, is this your actual room? Like not a guest room?" She looks surprised and I suddenly feel sheepish.

"Yeah, Annette wanted me to have my very own room. She tries to treat me nice since my mama really doesn't." I explain as she sets her bag on my desk then sits in the chair.

"Annette seems really nice." She looks at me. I sit on my bed.

"She is. I think it's because she's never had a kid of her own."

"Probably, but that's about to change." She laughs softly.

"Yeah, it'll be an adjustment." I smile.

"It sure will. I remember how it was after Cosmo was born and then Velma."

"At least it'll only be us three. You'll probably be over here a lot, too."

"Most likely. I enjoy being around you." She looks at me with a shy smile.

"I feel the same with you." I know I'm blushing.

"You look so kissable."

"Then kiss me."

10.

- -

It's basically an hour later and we're still kissing, but there's definitely less clothing. There's also music playing so it's not just us making noise. I don't know what exactly we're doing, but I'm happy with it. I can tell that Wednesday is, too. I hear the door open downstairs so we reluctantly stop and get dressed.

"If I walk in your room and y'all are naked, I'm so done!" Annette shouts causing me to blush and Wednesday to grin. Annette walks in with her eyes covered.

"How'd it go?" I ask as she sits on my desk chair.

"I honestly don't know. We talked, but mainly argued. Your mom was being quite stubborn which means that we're probably going to court."

"Wait, so she's actually trying to adopt you?" Wednesday asks.

"Yeah, it's gonna be a difficult process, but it'll be worth it." Annette grins.

"Hopefully, it will."

"It will. We're just gonna need proof that she's an unfit mother."

"I can help with that. My mom once saw Maureen get slapped across the face. She's also seen Maureen get dragged out of a car. I think she's even called Child Protection Services." Wednesday tells us.

"I remember both of those incidents."

"I've seen worse than that, but I'm pretty sure it'll all be considered heresy."

"Do they need proof that Maureen has been abused?" Wednesday looks at Annette.

"If they do then I definitely have scars."

"I don't know. I'll have to talk to my lawyer."

"We could like put a tiny camera in a shirt or something for proof like they do in those cop shows."

"But wouldn't I be hurt in the process?" I look at Wednesday.

"Yeah, I guess you would be." She sighs.

"We'll figure it out." Annette smiles then gets up.

"We should watch a movie later." I suggest.

"We should, but for now I'm gonna get some food ready." Annette leaves the room.

"This is an insane amount of courage that your aunt has."

"She's always been brave, never scared. She doesn't show fear it seems like."

"I can tell." Wednesday lays back down and I do the same.

I close my eyes and drift off to sleep. I start dreaming.

"Maureen Judith Baker!" I hear my mama yell, but I don't see her. I think I'm in my room back home.

"Yes, mama?" I reply and my vision becomes a bit clearer. I realize that I am in my room.

"I hate you!" She yells as she appears in my doorway.

"Stop!" I cover my ears, but my hands suddenly are tied to a chair. I look around and notice I'm in the basement all of a sudden.

"I'll fix you, honey. You'll be fixed, I promise." My mama gives me a sickly sweet grin.

"I don't need fixed!" I struggle against my restraints whilst I try and scream, but all that comes out is a hoarse whisper.

"Yes, you do. I'll fix you." She steps closer and I continue to struggle and attempt to scream.

"Mama, please!" My voice is a mere whisper and I don't even know if she heard it.

"Maureen, it'll be okay. You'll be normal again." I watch as grabs a wire or something and forces it into my head. I scream and she only laughs.

"Please, stop. I don't even like Wednesday anymore!" I lie.

"Yes, you do. You can't lie to me."

"I'm not lying. Please." She repeats the same thing from before.

"You deserve someone else, someone better. I'll help you."

"I don't want someone else. I want her." I make myself admit.

"No! You don't need her!"

"Yes, I do. She's the one for me. She's makes me so happy."

"No, she's made you happy!" With that, she does something and the wires start to shock me.

I jolt awake with a loud scream. Wednesday is already by my side. I cry onto her shoulder with the dream fresh in my mind. That dream made me realize how much I need Wednesday. I think I'm going to have to start thinking about who's more important to me, my mama or the girl who I'm falling for. It's sad that I have to decide, but it's all that I can think of.

"Do you wanna talk about it?" She asks as she looks at me.

"Not really, but it was about us in a way." I explain.

"I know. You kept saying my name. You sounded so scared."

"I was scared. That was a nightmare and I haven't one that bad in a while."

"It'll be okay. I'm here to protect you from whatever monster enters your dreams."

"It wasn't a monster, it was my mama. She was like one, though."

"I'll protect you from her, too. I'll protect you from anything, I promise." She reassures me.

"Thanks. I'd say the same, but I'm not really a fighter." I laugh and she does, too.

"I'll protect both of us, then." She grins and I get up.

"Good, you'll be the protector in this relationship." I cover my mouth instantly as I blush creeps up my neck.

"When were you going to tell me that we're dating?" She jokes.

"I think I've decided on right now." I reply in all seriousness.

"Really?" She grins happily.

"Yes, we're dating."

"That was simple. I'll take you on a date soon."

"I like the sound of that."

"I do, too." I go the bathroom and shut the door with a really big grin. I do what I need to do then walk back out.

"Annette wants us downstairs." She's already by the door so I walk over to her and we walk downstairs, holding hands.

"Are you finally dating or do I have to wait longer?" Annette asks when we get in the kitchen.

"You have to wait longer." I joke.

"Fuck, that really blows."

"She's joking, Annette."

"Yes! Yes! Yes! My ship has sailed!" Annette does a little dance making us laugh.

"Wow, you're embarrassing." I tell her.

"Eh, at least I'm funny. That makes up for it."

"Sure it does." I grin.

"Oh, hush it." We all grin, but our grins disappear when we hear a knock at the door.

"Girls, go upstairs. Okay?" I nod, but I'm confused. Wednesday grabs my hand and we head upstairs.

"C'mon." I lead her to the attic then to the little hidden room. I turn on the security cameras and see my mama and a police officer.

"Hello, ma'am, can we come in?" The officer asks in a polite voice.

"Um, sure." I see Annette move to the side to let them in.

"Where's my daughter?" My mama asks almost immediately.

"Not here. She's with Wednesday." Annette lies as she shuts the door.

"How do I know you aren't lying?" My mama looks around.

"I'll call Wednesday." Annette pulls out her phone and Wednesday does the same.

"Wait a couple seconds. Say we're at the movies or something."

"Got it." Annette calls and we wait til the last minute.

"Hello?" Wednesday whispers after I mute the cameras.

"Where are y'all?"

"Movies, why?"

"Just asking. When are you getting home?"

"Not sure yet."

"Well I'm gonna be making supper soon so can you be back in like an hour and a half."

"Sure. I have to go. We're annoying the bathroom users."

"Okay, see you guys in a bit."

"Mhm, bye." Wednesday hangs up and I turn the volume back up.

"See, not here."

"Well, I'm not trying to be the bad guy or anything, but technically Maureen needs to go back to her mom," The officer states.

"She doesn't want to be there. She'll be eighteen in almost a month. Can't you be a little lenient with her?" Annette pleads.

"It's not my decision, I'm sorry. She has to go back with her mom. You're not her legal guardian."

"Tell her to pack her stuff when she gets back. I want her home by eight." I watch my mama leave, but the officer stays.

"Do you know any good lawyers who deal with this kinda stuff?" Annette jokes.

"Yeah, my brother." The officer grins.

"So . . is he as hot as you or. .? Annette drags out the or then bites her lip.

"Why have him when you can have me?" I giggle as Annette blushes.

"We should interrupt them." Wednesday suggests. I nod as I turn off the cameras. We sneak down to the second floor then run down the stairs.

"Hello, my darling aunt. Who's this?" I ask with a grin.

"I thought you said they weren't here?" The officer asks.

"You didn't specify where here was." Annette replies.

"That's a good point." The officer looks at us.

"Thanks."

"Oh yeah . . my name's Theo Waverly." He holds out his hand for Wednesday and I. We shake it then step back.

"I better get going. I have a puppy at home and he gets scared if I'm not back by his supper time."

"Okay, I'll text you later."

"Bye!" Wednesday and I call out in a singsong voice.

"You two are embarrassing." Annette's face is a bit red, but she's smiling.

"Thanks, I know." Wednesday replies with a small smile on her face.

"Am I really going to have to go back home?" I look at Annette.

"Sadly . . yes. I can't go against the law."

"Ugh, this is absolutely ridiculous!" I whine stomping my foot.

"I'm right next door. Just scream really loudly if you need help. Someone will hear you."

"Exactly. And I'm a phone call away."

"I'm still scared."

"We won't let anything happen to you, baby girl." Wednesday grabs my hands and looks me in the eyes, "I promise." I smile at that.

□*□*□*□

"Okay, it's almost eight. I should take you home," Annette tells me.

"I wish Wednesday was still here," I admit.

"I know, but she had to leave before us." I nod as I grab my suitcase and duffle bag. I'm going to leave my journal and books here even though I don't to.

"I think I'm ready." I feel so nervous and I hope that it won't be that bad.

"If you say so." We walk out to her car and then get in.

The drive seems to go by quickly, almost too quickly. I hate it and wish it could of lasted longer, but at the same time I don't. I know I need to just get over it, but my mama is scary when she's angry. She's like a monster and I know it'll be like that.

"I love you, Maureen."

"I love you, too Annette. I'll call you tomorrow." I reply with a weak smile.

"Or tonight. Call me if you need anything."

"I will. Night." I don't let her say anything else cause I get out. I grab my stuff then slowly walk to the front door.

"Hello, Maureen," My mama says after she opens the door.

"Hi, mama." I try and smile, but fail miserably.

"Set your stuff upstairs then come down. We need to talk about this issue." She exaggerates issue which frustrates me, but I won't say anything. She's also eerily calm.

"Okay." I take my time getting upstairs and putting my stuff in my room.

I look at my outfit and immediately regret it. I know my mama is going to say something about it. I have a light green crop top on and it is only inches under my chest. At least my pants aren't that bad, they're light gray joggers. I like it, but it's definitely not something I should wear around my mama. I take my time going downstairs, not wanting to deal with my mama.

"Come to the dining room." I do that and she's sitting there with her legs crossed. She just stares at me and I start to feel uncomfortable.

"What do you want to talk about?" I ask.

"You . . which should be pretty obvious. You've made a mistake and I'm going to help you." She says it like it's so clear to her, like she understands.

"There's nothing wrong with me. I like Wednesday, but that doesn't mean anything. What if I'm bisexual?" I question.

"You can't be. It just doesn't work like that, Maureen. I went through this with your aunt and she got better."

"Well it didn't last. That's probably because it's not a disease like you think. It's nothing like that." I feel anger surge through me when she shakes her head.

"Maureen! Stop this! You are not a lesbian or even bisexual!" Now we're both angry which can't be a good thing.

"No, I won't stop this! I love her and you can't stop me from loving her!" I slam my fists on the table.

"It's not love, Maureen!"

"You can't tell me what love is! I'm almost eighteen, I should be able to make my own decisions!" This has turned into a shouting match and I plan on winning.

"You're still young! I didn't know what love was until I met your father and guess what happened . .he left me?! Wednesday will do the same!"

"You're just upset that my father left you! That's the only reason!"

"I don't want you to end up like me! It's not fun!"

"Don't try and predict my future! I know what's going to be best for me and that's Wednesday . . it'll always be her." I calm down just a bit.

"You're a sinner! You're a goddamned sinner." She mutters the last part, but I still hear her.

"I'd rather be a sinner than lie to myself."

"No!" She stands up quickly and steps towards me. I move quickly so she doesn't get to me.

"What are you doing?" I make my way to the door as quick as possible, but it's locked.

"You can't leave . . not until you're fixed!"

My nightmare from earlier is coming alive and I'm terrified as hell . . .

12.

"Mama!" I yell. I've been locked in the basement the whole night.

"Shut up! You can't come out of there until you've changed your mind!" My mama yells back.

"Then I'll stay down here for a long time! This won't do anything!" I bang my fists against the door one last time then sit on the steps.

"It will, I know it will." I hear her say and I shake my head.

"Whatever you want to believe." I reply.

I hear her footsteps walk away and I smile. I'll just have to wait a bit longer so that I can go through with my plan. Maybe my mama will leave, all I need is five minutes. I don't even think it'll take that long. I guess I won't know until I do it.

I sit on the steps for a while longer. I'm getting bored and tired, but I have to wait until she isn't in the kitchen. I listen carefully to her movements and try to figure out what she's doing. I can't really tell, but I'm pretty sure that she's cooking. She does that when she's upset or nervous, it's a stress reliever for her.

"Maureen, I have to go to the store. I'll be back in ten minutes." I smile then reply back with an okay.

I wait until I hear the car leave the driveway then wait another minute. I get up and carefully walk down the steps, cringing at every creak that the stairs make. I go to the window and open it a little bit. I take a deep breath then look behind me one last time before I start yelling for help. Luckily, the window is close to the side of Wednesday's house.

"Maureen?" Her mama asks from the kitchen window.

"Help me," I plead and she nods.

"Dale! Come quick!" She looks back to me with a smile.

"What is it?" I see him appear which is all it takes.

"Get Raph then send him over. I'll try and get in." He runs out the door and disappears to the front of my house.

"Oh my God. Maureen, are you okay?" Wednesday comes out a minute later with Raphael behind her. He goes to the front of my house to try and help his daddy.

"I'm scared. She'll be back soon." I reply.

"We'll get you out and if we can't, we'll call the cops." She reassures me.

"But what if that doesn't work?" Tears form in my eyes.

"It will, baby girl." Her smile calms me down a little.

"Dad got in!" I hear Raph yell.

"Go to the steps. I'll be at the door." I nod then run to the steps. The door opens seconds later.

"Where's your bags from yesterday?" Raph asks.

"In my room. I didn't have a chance to unpack." I tell him.

"Get her out. I'll get the bags." I walk with Raph outside and Wednesday immediately pulls me into her arms.

"You'll be okay." We walk back to her house.

"Have you had something to eat?" Their mama asks when we walk in.

"No, I haven't." I reply in a quiet voice.

"I'll make you something. Pancakes?" I nod as their daddy comes back.

"Here you go." He hands me my stuff.

"Thanks, Mr. Kinsley."

"We should call your aunt." Wednesday tells me so I nod then grab my stuff. We head to her room.

"Hi, Wednesday. What's up?" I hear the nervousness in my aunt's voice.

"Hey, it's actually Maureen." I reply.

"What happened?"

"I got locked in the basement for the whole night. Luckily, my mama left so I opened the window and yelled for help. I'm fine, now." I explain as I yawn.

"Shit, I didn't expect that to happen. She probably had some type of plan."

"Maybe .. but it doesn't matter anymore. I got out and now I have no idea what to do."

"Uhm, I'll send Theo over to get you then we'll go from there."

"Okie dokie. I'll be waiting."

"Bring Wednesday. Have her pack a bag, too."

"Alright, how much stuff should she pack?"

"As much as she can. I'll come with Theo so I can talk to her parents."

"Uhm, I'll tell her."

"Okay, bye." She hangs up quickly.

"What's happening?" Wednesday asks.

"Annette and Theo are coming over. She's gonna talk to your parents."

"I'll go and tell them. You stay here and lay down, okay?" I nod then lay down.

I immediately feel tired and almost close my eyes. I hear yelling from upstairs, but I ignore it for a couple seconds. Then I realize that the voice is my mama. She's accusing them of taking me, but they keep denying it. Raph comes in the room and sits next to me.

"C'mon, I promise you won't have to face her." He reaches out his hand and I grab it.

"Where are we going?" I whisper to him.

"Away, out of this fucking town." He grabs my suitcase and I grab my duffle bag then we make our way to his room.

"Who's going first?" I ask as we stand in front of his tiny window.

"You. I have another way out. Just take the bags." I nod then he helps me out. I'm handed the bags then I watch him close the window and walk away.

I see Raphael appear a minute later. He grabs my hand and I follow him as quickly as I can. I wish I was with Wednesday, but I guess she can't be here.

We end up in an alleyway with a car waiting. The girl in the front seat is unfamiliar.

"Ready?" She asks as I get in the back and Raph gets in the passenger's seat.

"Yeah, we're ready." She speeds off and I watch as Raph grabs her hand.

"I'm Trina. Formally known as Trent." She smiles at me then turns around.

"Hi?" I'm confused as to what she meant.

"She used to be a boy, but now she's a girl . . my girl." Raph smiles happily.

"Oh, I've never heard of anything like that before." I reply.

"Wow, she really was sheltered." Trina shakes her head.

"And now she likes Wednesday. It's funny how things work out." Raph responds.

"So true."

I lay my head against the window. All I can think about is Wednesday, the girl who changed my life in a matter of days. How is that even possible when all she did was look at me? She didn't even have to talk to me or even smile at me. I knew that I needed her the second I saw her.

I hope Wednesday and I are beside each other in a couple years. I hope we stick together and we never have to let go of each other. I hope that we don't have to say goodbye to one another because I don't think I could handle that. I hope I don't have to worry about losing her.

I'd push everyone away to be with Wednesday. She what makes me happy, she's what I want most. If she became the only one who cares, I'd be fine with that. I don't know how or why she makes me feel this way, but she does. Am I crazy for thinking that?

"We're here."

13.

I look around at my surroundings. We're in a woodsy area which means that we could be close to town but also very far away. The house is decent looking on the outside and it almost looks abandoned. There's two stories and I think an attic, but who's house is it?

"Where are we?" I ask.

"Our place in a way," Trina responds.

"This is where we come to get away," Raphael adds.

"How far away?"

"An hour and a half away. You fell asleep on the way here."

"Oh, alrighty."

"Let's get out." Trina and Raph get out first then I follow.

"You'll be here until things calm down." Raph tells me as we walk in.

The place is nicer than I expected and really clean. The wallpaper and furniture are definitely outdated, but it doesn't look that bad. The living room is on one side and the kitchen is on the other side do the downstairs.

I notice a sun room towards the back, it seems to circle to the side of the kitchen. There also seems to be a bathroom underneath the stairs.

"Your room is upstairs. I'll show you while Raph makes food." Trina smiles at me.

"Okie dokie." I respond as she grabs a bag for me. I grab the other one and we head upstairs.

"You'll have your own bathroom which might be helpful when we have people over." She opens the door and my eyes widen as we set the bags down.

The room is way different than the rest of the house. The bed is on a platform with a two-shelf bookcase underneath along with what appears to be a T.V. stand in the front of it. The walls have splattered paint which actually looks pretty neat. There's two windows with matching tie-dye curtains. The closet has a sliding door, but instead of a normal door, it's mirrors.

"I know it's a little out there, but you'll get used to it."

"I actually really like it. It is out there, but not in a bad way." I explain and she grins.

"I like you. You're not afraid to tell the truth."

"Thanks . . I think."

"Food is ready!" Raph yells as he bangs pots and pans together.

"Let's go." We walk down to the kitchen. I forget to tell you about the door to the kitchen, they look like something out of a western.

"I made grilled cheese sandwiches because it was easy and simple." I notice that the sun room and kitchen are connected by a French door.

"They smell great." I tell him.

"They do." Trina comments as we walk to the table which is right next to the sun room windows.

I wait for them to eat to take a bite. It tastes really good, but that could be because I haven't eaten in a while. I slowly eat the rest even though I want to devour the whole thing in seconds. I take a sip of fruit punch and notice that Raph and Trina are looking at me.

"What?" I look at them.

"You're so polite like how?" Trina asks me.

"I was raised this way." I shrug, not really sure what I should say.

"Wow, your mom really was strict." Raph shakes his head in almost a shocked manner.

"I guess."

"Let's finish so you can get settled in. We have to leave, but only for a while."

"You'll lock the door, right?" I finish as quickly as possible, not caring anymore.

"Of course. The sun room is a little open so you might want to avoid that." Raph advises.

"I'll just stay upstairs."

"That's probably best." Trina smiles then gets up. Raph does the same then he grabs the empty dishes. I grab my cup then watch him put the dishes in the sink.

"We'll be back." Raph tells me as we all walk to the foyer.

"Will Wednesday be with you?"

"Possibly." Trina looks at me.

"Okie dokie."

"Bye, Maureen." They leave and I wait for the door to lock then head to my room.

I make my way upstairs carefully, not wanting to spill my drink. I walk into my room and lock the door behind me. I set my drink down then check to see if my windows are locked. I even check the bathroom window which isn't big enough for a person to fit through. I'm just paranoid because of my mama and I really want Wednesday here.

I decide to take a shower because of the night I had. I pick out an some pajamas and set them on the bed then go to the bathroom. I turn on the shower and then strip down to nothing. I jump in and take my time cleaning myself. I get out and also take my time getting dressed again.

I notice the T.V. again, but decide to unpack instead. I only have what fit in the bag which seems to be a lot. I take my time doing that so I won't be as bored. I smile at the clothes, remembering the day I got them which was honestly one of my favorite days. I set the bags on the top shelf of the closet then lay on my new, temporary bed.

□*□*□*□

"Babygirl!" I hear someone exclaim.

"Mhm, I'm sleeping," I reply.

"It's Wednesday, though." I immediately smile.

"I'm up." I open my eyes and she's sitting right beside me.

"How long have you been asleep?"

"What time is it?"

"Almost six."

"I fell asleep at like eleven so there's your answer." I grin and she grins back.

"Raph and Trina are having a party tonight. They've been planning it for like a month so they're not going to cancel it, but we can stay up here."

"Sounds good, but I'm hungry."

"Let's go get something to eat."

"Hey, get what you want now cause the party starts at eight." Trina warns.

"Obviously." Wednesday rolls her eyes then grabs the tortilla chips.

"Not those." Trina grabs those from her hand.

"Then what are we supposed to eat? And don't say pizza."

"I dunno. Just not the chips or salsa or the cheese dip."

"Whatever, Trina." Trina walks away with the chips, putting them somewhere. Wednesday grabs the cheese puffs, strawberries, whipped cream, pepperonis, and two water bottles along with two Dr. Pepper bottles.

"Should we hurry?" I look at all the stuff.

"After I find something healthy, but go quickly." She hands me the cheese puffs, pepperonis, and the drinks then I rush upstairs.

I set everything on my bed then set up pillows and blankets on the front of the platform part of the bed. I make it look nice then decide to make sure it's comfy; it is. I get the comforter and put it on the built-in T.V. stand to make it like a fort. The last thing I do is make room for the food. I finish up as Wednesday walks in.

"This is so cool!" She exclaims as I notice that she has a medium sized bowl full of mixed fruit instead of just strawberries. I also see that she got peanut butter.

"Thanks, I tried." I grin then I set the food up. We crawl in and we both fit comfortably.

"This is really nice. I love it." She kisses my forehead then we start eating.

14.

"**F**uck yes!" Someone shouts from downstairs, waking us both up.

"Ugh, this was romantic and cute, but now it's kinda ruined," Wednesday tells me with a frown as she looks at her phone. I see that the time is 3 in the morning. We've been woken up at least every hour.

"I can fix that." I pull her in for a kiss.

I lay back down and she gets on top of me. We continue kissing each other, trying to ignore the party downstairs. We pull back when we hear a loud thud on the door. It seems that it was just someone being stupid, but I soon realize that I'm wrong.

"Wednesday, come downstairs," Some guy slurs.

"No, go away!" Wednesday shouts at him.

"C'mon, I haven't seen you in ages." The guy practically whines.

"There's a reason for that, Simon!" She yells back.

"That was a while ago. It shouldn't even matter!" He hits the door really hard causing it to shake.

"Fuck off!"

"Wednesday!" He pounds on the door repeatedly.

"Just ignore him." I tell her as quietly as possible.

"Oh, that's why I can't come in. There's a girl in there." He stops causing her to look worried.

"No, you can't come in because you can't keep your hands to yourself!" She gets angry and stands up.

"It was a mistake. I was drunk, you were drunk . . things happened." My eyes widen when he says this.

"No, you got me drunk. I was fifteen and you should of known better." She puts emphasis on you both times and I start to understand what happened.

"I thought you liked me. I was nineteen at the time and I've only been with like three girls, but none of them made me happy. You did, though." He explains and she scoffs.

"Yeah, fucking right."

"I'm telling the truth, Nes."

"Don't call me that. You don't get to call me that . . ever again!" She kicks the door as if it'll help.

"But you used to love it. That made your beautiful green eyes light up."

"Not anymore, Simon. I hate it!" She kicks the door again.

"Stop lying, baby! Please just let me in or at least come out here." He begs and it's honestly so pathetic to me.

"No, no, and no." She glares at the door.

"Whatever, you'll come crawling back . . they all do." We listen as his steps fade away then look at each other with a grin.

"How long will this last?" I look at her and she shrugs.

"Probably til morning. Then they'll be here all day sleeping."

"Dang, that's gonna suck."

"Yeah, but we'll order a pizza. I have an idea on how we'll get it up here without going down there."

"I hope it works . . whatever it is." I grin then yawn.

"Let's go back to sleep. Maybe we'll actually be able to."

□*□*□*□

"Is this even going to work?" I ask Wednesday.

"Of course it is," She responds with a grin.

"I'll probably be bad at this. I've never done this before," The pizza girl yells.

"Just put the pizza in the basket and we'll lift it up." Wednesday shouts back.

The girl nods, but she's clearly nervous. Wednesday ties a rope to the door then ties a knot around the handle of the basket. She throws in thirty dollars then slowly moves it to the girl. The girl takes the money then puts the pizza in. We pull it back up then thank her.

"That was easy." I pull the pizza out and set it on the bed.

"I do it all the time. I usually have this one guy, but he was sick today." She takes a slice and I do the same.

"Wednesday!" Trina shouts.

"How are they even up? It's one in the afternoon." We finish our slices then head downstairs.

"Hey, Nes," Simon Says with a smirk.

"Did you order pizza?" Raph asks ignoring Simon.

"We were hungry." She explains.

"Next time . . don't be so selfish. Also put some clothes on." We look down and I honestly don't see a problem.

"We do have clothes on." I gesture to both of us as if I'm proving a point.

"Short shorts and baggy shirts aren't the greatest outfit." Trina rolls her eyes.

"They're pajamas, not an actual outfit." Wednesday glares at her.

"I see nothing wrong with their outfits. They look pretty hot." Simon gives us a look that I don't quite like.

"Shut up! We didn't ask you!" Wednesday yells at him.

"Wednesday! That's our friend." Raph scolds her, but I can tell that she doesn't care.

"Well, ask him about two summers ago then see if he's still your friend." She crosses her arms, obviously not letting up on her brother scolding her.

"Nes, you said that you wouldn't say anything." Simon looks worried and everybody is staring at him, six people to be exact and that's not including Wednesday and I.

"I changed my mind." She has a smug look on her face.

"Simon, what is she talking about?" Raph looks at him with anger in his eyes.

"I honestly have no idea. I can't even think of anything." He's lying to Raph and I think everybody knows.

"Come on, stop lying! You know what you did!" Wednesday stomps her foot and glares at him.

"It wasn't wrong. You're acting like I raped you, I only felt you up!"

"You did what to my sister?!" Raph says.

"You stuck your hand down my shorts and tried to do more, but someone was knocking on the door! I was fifteen for God's sake!" She yells almost immediately after Raph speaks.

"What the hell? Get the fuck out of here!" Raph goes to push him out, but Trina stops him.

"Stop, you're acting childish!" Trina yells at him.

"Trina, did you not hear what he did?" He glares at her and I can tell that this isn't gonna end well.

"Yes, but it was a mistake. He obviously didn't mean to." She's defending Simon which is absolutely ridiculous to me.

"Both of you, get the fuck out!" Raph points to the door.

"Baby, don't do this." Trina begs.

"I'll do whatever the hell I want. That includes breaking up with you!" Wednesday looks at her brother with a shocked look.

"No! You can't!"

"Yes, I can! Go date Simon!"

"Fine, but good luck with finding someone who actually cares about you like I did . . I bet you won't." Trina walks out and Simon reluctantly follows.

"Anybody who still wants to be friends with them, get out." I watch as everybody else grabs their stuff them leaves.

"We'll find you new friends, better friends."

"I have y'all." Raph smiles, but I can tell he's very upset.

"You want to eat pizza and watch horror movies?"

15.

"Hi, I'm Jaina Deveit," A girl with light blonde hair and hazel eyes says with a nervous smile.

It's been three days since Raph lost all his friends. Wednesday felt bad so she went out and tried to find willing participants to audition. We've met at least thirty-seven people, including Jaina. We have at least ten more or at least that's what Wednesday told us.

"Hi, tell us about yourself." Wednesday smiles as the girl starts talking about herself.

I look at her appearance as she speaks. Her blonde hair has a blue streak on the right side. It kind of matches her tight white crop top that has a rainbow on it. Her skirt is leather and so are the knee-high boots. The only make-up she has on is blue lipstick and heavy eyeliner which actually doesn't look bad.

"Thanks, we'll call if you've been picked." Wednesday waves at her as she leaves.

"I liked her style." Raph comments when she leaves the house.

"Me too." I reply.

"What about her as a friend?" She gives us both a disapproving look.

"Her top five bands are great, along with her top five favorite movies. I liked her eyes, too."

"So she's a possibility?"

"Yeah, so that makes seven possibles, right?" He asks as she puts Jaina's picture in the possibility pile.

"Correct."

"Who's next?" I ask.

"I dunno. Next!" A guy walks in.

"Hi, I'm Tobi." He looks confident unlike most everybody else.

"Hey, Tobi." Raph actually looks happy and interested with Tobi.

"This is good." Wednesday whispers and I know that she's noticed.

As Tobi and Raph talk, I focus on Tobi. He's the cliche bad boy type, but I don't think Raph cares. Tobi has the tattoos, the piercings, and the leather jacket on him. I just hope that he is actually nice cause Raph deserves that right about now. They finish speaking, but I know that they want to continue.

"We should hang out sometime." Raph tells him with a shy grin.

"Yeah, we should. What are you doing later?"

"Whatever you can plan within five hours." Raph smirks at him.

"Mhm, I can plan a lot. I'll need your number, though." They're both smirking and blushing.

"Here." Raph hands him the number then Tobi leaves.

"I don't even need to ask about him." We at least need another friend and there's like six more."

"So, who did you decide on anybody?" Wednesday asks Raph after we finish.

"Jaina and Tobi."

"Alrighty, sounds good."

"I feel bad for everybody else," I say.

"They can make friends with someone else that came here."

"Good point. Gimme Jaina's number."

"You should shower soon. Your date is in almost four hours." She tells him.

"I'll do it after I call that chick."

"If you need anything, we'll be in our room." We head upstairs.

We lay on the bed and I close my eyes. My eyes open suddenly when I hear a loud yelp. I look to see Wednesday already getting up and I follow behind her. We go to Raph's room and he's on the floor in a puddle of blood. I scream as Wednesday kneels down to check his pulse.

"He's alive. Call the cops!" She shouts with tears streaming down her face. "Okay. Hold on!" I run to her room, grabbing her phone. I call 911 as I run back to Raph's room.

Wednesday tells me the address for the operator. I quickly explain the situation then give the operator the house's address. He tells me the cops should be here soon with an ambulance. I thank him then hang up.

"They'll be here as soon as they can." I tell her and she punches the floor.

"As soon as they can?! What the fuck is that supposed to mean?! My brother is goddamned dying and they're taking their time getting here!" She yells, scaring me.

"Wednesday, please calm down." I beg and she looks away.

"I can't lose him . . I just can't." She mumbles, looking at him.

"I know, but he'll get help soon." I reassure her, kneeling next to her.

"Nes . . ." Raph whispers.

"What's wrong?"

"I love you. You're the best sister anyone could of asked for. Please don't let this get to you. You're strong, you always have been." He weakly smiles at her.

"I love you, but you don't need to talk like this."

"Just in case." I hear loud knocking on the front door so I run downstairs.

"Hi, he's upstairs." The paramedics follow behind me then I watch them help Raph on to the gurney.

"Do you know what happened?" The female paramedic asks Wednesday.

"No, we heard him yelp. We came running, but he was already in a puddle of blood." Wednesday explains as we get in the back of the ambulance.

"There seems to be a stab wound." The male paramedic tells us.

"How could that of even happened?" I question, looking at Wednesday as the ambulance starts moving.

□*□*□*□

"Raphael will be fine. He needs to rest right now, but you can see him later," The doctor tells Wednesday and I.

"So the surgery went okay?" Wednesday asks quickly.

"Yes, it went great. It was long and somewhat difficult, but he's all patched up." She smiles at us.

"Good, good. How much longer will we need to wait?" Wednesday asks the doctor, biting her lip.

"Maybe an hour. I'll have a nurse let you know."

"Thanks." Wednesday smiles at the doctor, but glares at her as she walks away.

"You should call your parents now." I tell Wednesday.

"Only if you go find me some coffee." She replies with pouted lips.

"Deal."

I wait until Wednesday dials her mom's number to go get coffee. I head to the place in the lobby. I order her favorite thing then mine and I finally pay. I make my way back upstairs when I see security running towards the elevators. I worry as I wait for the elevator, hoping Wednesday didn't try anything. I'm confused when I don't see her sitting in the same spot as before.

I then see Wednesday fighting with a security guard, obviously succeeding. I drop the coffees as I run toward her, not caring about them anymore. Security guards are surrounding her and I try to push past them. One of them yells at me to move, but I ignore him. Suddenly, I feel something hit my neck and I fall to the ground, blackness clouding my eyes.

16.

"She's been like this for nine months, what are you doing to solve this?" I hear someone ask.

"Ms. Baker, we're doing everything we can, but —" Another voice tells the first voice.

"It's obviously not enough! My daughter is still here and she still likes females!" I look and see a familiar face and then another face that I don't quite recognize.

"We're not concerned about that at this moment in time. She still needs to recover from the accident." I see Mina glare at the woman.

"That abomination caused this!" The woman slaps Mina and I gasp.

"Mina!" I exclaim, running to her.

"I'm alright, Maureen. Go sit back down." Mina smiles at me, trying to reassure me, but it doesn't work.

"Who is she?" I ask Mina quietly.

"What do you mean by that?" The woman asks, looking hurt.

"Should I know her?" I look at Mina with a raised eyebrow.

"Not yet. You've had some trouble remembering things and she's just here to check up on you."

"I thought Annette was supposed to do that." I feel confused and I try not to show it.

"She is, but this lady does, too. Her name's Laurel."

"Hi, Laurel." I hold out my hand for her to shake, but she lets out a frustrated groan and continues to look very hurt.

"I have to go now." The lady now known as Laurel walks out the door.

"Can Annette visit today?" I plead, needing a familiar face.

"I don't know . . . you're only allowed one visitor per day."

"But I don't know that lady. She shouldn't count!" I exclaim.

"Fine, but only for a little bit."

□*□*□*□

I wait patiently for Annette, knowing she'll be here soon. Annette has visited me almost three times a week since I've got here. She won't tell me why I'm here, but I wish she would. Everybody knows why I'm here, but they won't tell me anything. All I know is that I had an accident that put me here.

I'm eighteen so I could technically check myself out, but I haven't done that, yet. I've been here for a while and I think I'm getting better. Mina thinks I'll be almost completely okay within three or four months. I hope so because this place can be quite boring to me. Annette has told me multiple times that I can go live with her once I get out.

I like that idea a lot. Annette is really nice and she's fun to hang out with. Sometimes she brings a girl with her who's just as nice. The girl's name is Wednesday and she's supposedly my best friend. I don't remember her at all, but I trust that they are telling me the truth.

I don't remember much from before the accident, but I'm starting to remember more and more everyday. I know my name, how old I am, and when I was born which are the most important things to me. I know that Annette is my aunt, but I have barely have any clue who my mother is. Wednesday is one of my best friends along with her brother who can't visit because he's in the hospital. I hope that Wednesday is telling me the truth about her brother because it's nice to think that I have more than one friend.

"Maureen!" Annette exclaims when she sees me. We hug like usual.

"Hi, Annette." I pull away with a grin on my face.

"Wednesday and I brought someone with us. Want to meet them?" Annette asks and I nod.

"Of course." I feel excited and nervous. Meeting new people has been a challenge for me lately, but I'm getting used to it.

"She says it's okay." Annette tells someone in the hallway.

Wednesday appears in the room with a guy. The guy looks very familiar and I assume that he's her brother, my other best friend. He's limping a bit and I wonder why. Maybe that's why he was in the hospital.

"Hi, Maureen. How are you?" He asks sitting down. I sit on the opposite side of the table.

"I'm good, how are you?"

"I'm amazing. Do you remember me?" He looks hopeful when he asks the question so I try my hardest to figure it out.

"Raphael?" I bite my lip nervously, hoping I'm right.

"Damn, how the hell did you figure that out so quick?" Wednesday asks with a laugh as she sits across from me.

"I dunno, but I'm starting to regain my memory." I shrug, feeling proud.

"That's awesome." Annette sits beside me and I try to nod, but I suddenly feel very strange.

My head starts pounding and I feel dizzy like I'm in a tornado or something. I grip onto the table, trying to focus on the face in front of me. I hear voices and I see a rush of movement beside me, but I don't know what exactly is going on. I fall back, not able to control my actions anymore. Someone picks me up and puts my head in their lap, but I can't see the person's face. I start to get flashbacks.

17.

- -

"My darling daughter, come here!" A singsong voice calls out and I watch a young girl run down a flight of stairs with a grin on her face.

"Daddy!" She shouts, jumping into a man's arms.

"How was your day, my dear?" He looks at her, with a happy grin.

"It was amazing! Like really amazing!" The girl tells him.

"I'm glad it hear that. Where's mommy?" He looks confused, but also quite angry.

"She's having one of her special naps." The little girl whispers to him and his jaw clenches as he sets her down.

"Go play outside. I'll come and get you in a little while."

"Okay, daddy."

The little girl skips to the backdoor then skips outside. She goes to the swingset and sits down, but keeps her eyes focused on an upstairs window. Suddenly, the curtains open and the dad is standing there, his back facing her. She hears a loud noise like someone yelling, but she can't make it out. A woman appears close to the window, trying to shut the curtains, but the man stops her.

"What the fuck are you doing?" The woman yells, pushing the man roughly.

"You cannot be asking that right now, Laurie. You're supposed to be hugging our daughter, not a beer bottle!" The man yells back.

"She's fine. I made her breakfast!" The woman takes a drink out of a bottle.

"It's almost six in the evening!" He grabs the bottle from her and throws it on the wall, causing glass and liquid to go everywhere.

"Fuck off, Bernard! I'm a grown woman and I can do whatever the hell I want!" The woman slaps him and he just turns to walk away.

"I'm leaving and I'm taking Maureen with me."

"You will not!" She tries to stop him, but he ignores her.

"I am. This isn't a good environment for her."

"Over my dead body!"

"Fine, but I'll be back."

□*□*□*□

"Mommy, where's daddy?" The same little girl from before asks.

"He went away," The woman answers.

"When will he be back?" The girl is clearly upset.

"I don't know, honey. He left when you were one and a half."

"But I'm four now. Shouldn't he be back by now?"

"Shush. I'm done talking about it. Ask again and I'll spank you."

□*□*□*□

"Mommy, is daddy coming home? It's been a long time and he's missed my fifth birthday and my sixth one," The girl states as she eats a spoonful of cereal.

"No, he's not! Stop asking!" The woman shouts, causing the little girl to drop her spoon.

"But he's my daddy. He's supposed to be here." The girl presses on.

"Enough, Maureen!" The woman backhands the little girl very hard, causing the girl to shriek and fall out of her chair.

□*□*□*□

"Why can't I have friends?" The little girl asks her mother as they pull in a driveway.

"Because you don't need them," The woman responds.

"Why not? I'm almost ten."

"Stop asking questions." They get out.

"But Mama . . I want friends. Everybody at church has friends."

The woman walks around to the side of the car. The daughter stops in her tracks, fear in her eyes. The girl closes her eyes, waiting for something.

"Open your eyes. You need to see your punishment." With that, the woman backhands the girl causing the girl to fall to the ground.

"Ow, mama. Why'd you do that?" The girl is crying and her right cheek is turning red.

"Shut up and get inside."

□*□*□*□

"Mama, why did we leave church early?" The girl is older, maybe fourteen.

"You know why, Maureen," The woman responds.

"I was just talking to him." The girl mumbles.

"What was that?" The woman angrily yells.

"I was just talking to him." The girl repeats in a shaky voice.

"You were flirting, acting slutty! That's not just talking!" The woman gets out then walks to the other side.

"Mama, please!" The girl pleads as the woman opens the door.

"I'll teach you how to be appropriate! Get out!"

"No, please!" The girl's hair is grabbed and she's pulls out of the car by her hair.

She fights against it, but the woman is stronger. The woman continues yelling at the poor girl. There's a voice in the distance, shouting at the woman. The girl is dragged into the house and then it ends.

□*□*□*□

"You can't stop me from seeing her!" A girl screams.

I realize that the girl is me. It was always me. All these flashbacks are of me. I'm regaining my memory!

"You're in the hospital because of her!" The woman yells and I realize it's Laurel.

"So what? She's the best thing that has ever happened to me!" The girl now known as myself yells.

"You little fucking bitch! How could you do this to me?"

"I'm in love with Wednesday . . that's how!"

"You'll regret thinking that." Everything goes black after that.

I regain conciseness and see all the familiar faces around me. I start crying, overwhelmed with everything. My mama put me here all because of my sexuality, but how did she make me forget almost everything about my life? I reach for Annette, needing a hug from her. I sob uncontrollably into her shoulder as more memories flood my mind.

"It's going to be okay, sweetie." Annette rubs my shoulder, trying to soothe me.

"My dad didn't leave us. He didn't want to leave me, but my mama made him go without me." I state, suddenly pulling away.

"What? How do you know that?" Raph asks.

"I got a flashback to the day he left. They argued about my mama's alcohol problem."

"Laurel didn't have an alcohol problem. I know that for a fact." Annette seems so sure and I hate that.

"She did, I'm not lying. What's my dad's last name?"

"Um, I think Shuemen."

"I have to find him."

"You don't even know where to start. How do you expect to find him?"

"I have a couple ideas, but I need to get out of here."

"Let's go. You're eighteen now."